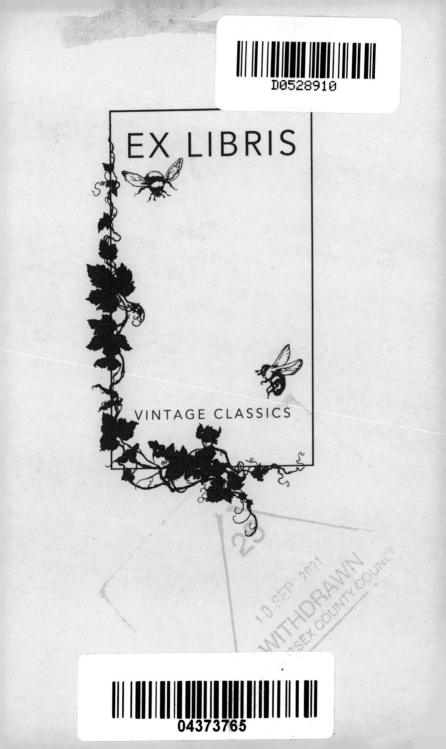

EX LIBRIS

VINTAGE CLASSICS

MRS DALLOWAY'S PARTY

Virginia Woolf was born in London in 1882, the daughter of Sir Leslie Stephen, first editor of *The Dictionary of National Biography*. After his death in 1904 Virginia and her sister, the painter Vanessa Bell, moved to Bloomsbury and became the centre of 'The Bloomsbury Group'. This informal collective of artists and writers, which included Lytton Strachey and Roger Fry, exerted a powerful influence over early twentieth-century British culture.

In 1921 Virginia married Leonard Woolf, a writer and social reformer. Three years later, her first novel, *The Voyage Out*, was published, followed by *Night and Day* (1919) and *Jacob's Room* (1922). These first novels show the development of Virginia Woolf's distinctive and innovative narrative style. It was during this time that she and Leonard Woolf founded The Hogarth Press with the publication of the co-authored *Two Stories* in 1917, hand-printed in the dining room of their house in Surrey.

Between 1925 and 1931 Virginia Woolf produced what are now regarded as her finest masterpieces, from *Mrs Dalloway* (1925) to the poetic and highly experimental novel *The Waves* (1931). She also maintained an astonishing output of literary criticism, short fiction, journalism and biography, including the playfully subversive *Orlando* (1928) and *A Room of One's Own* (1929), a passionate feminist essay. This intense creative productivity was often matched by periods of mental illness, from which she had suffered since her mother's death in 1895. On 28 March, 1941, a few months before the publication of her final novel, *Between the Acts*, Virginia Woolf committed suicide.

ALSO BY VIRGINIA WOOLF

Novels

The Voyage Out

Night and Day

Jacob's Room

Mrs Dalloway

To the Lighthouse

Orlando

The Years

The Waves

Between the Acts

Shorter fiction

A Haunted House: The Complete Shorter Fiction

Non-Fiction and Other Works

Flush

Roger Fry

A Room of One's Own and *Three Guineas*

The Common Reader Vols 1 and 2

Selected Diaries (edited by Anne Olivier Bell)

Selected Letters (edited by Joanne Trautmann Banks)

VIRGINIA WOOLF

Mrs Dalloway's Party

A Short Story Sequence

EDITED AND WITH AN INTRODUCTION BY
Stella McNichol

VINTAGE BOOKS
London

Published by Vintage 2012

2 4 6 8 10 9 7 5 3 1

First published in Great Britain by The Hogarth Press in 1973

Published by Vintage in 2010

Vintage
Random House, 20 Vauxhall Bridge Road,
London SW1V 2SA

www.vintage-classics.info

Addresses for companies within The Random House Group Limited
can be found at: www.randomhouse.co.uk/offices.htm

The Random House Group Limited Reg. No. 954009

A CIP catalogue record for this book
is available from the British Library

ISBN 9780099541325

The Random House Group Limited supports The Forest Stewardship
Council (FSC®), the leading international forest certification
organisation. Our books carrying the FSC label are printed on FSC®
certified paper. FSC is the only forest certification scheme endorsed
by the leading environmental organisations, including Greenpeace.
Our paper procurement policy can be found at:
www.randomhouse.co.uk/environment

Printed and bound in Great Britain by Clays Ltd, St Ives Plc

Contents

Acknowledgments

I wish to acknowledge my indebtedness:

to Quentin and Angelica Bell for permission to quote from the Virginia Woolf MSS;

to Quentin Bell for his help and interest in my work on the Dalloway MSS;

to the Curator for the Berg Collection of the New York Public Library for assistance and permission to consult the Virginia Woolf MSS in that collection;

to the Hogarth Press for permission to quote the four stories: *The Man Who Loved His Kind*, *Together and Apart*, *The New Dress* and *A Summing Up*, from *A Haunted House and Other Short Stories*;

and finally to the University of Newcastle upon Tyne for the award of the Sir James Knott Fellowship which made the research possible.

Introduction

WHILE WORKING ON the Mrs Dalloway MSS, in order primarily to establish a first draft version of that novel, I became aware of Virginia Woolf's preoccupation with a particular social occasion, the party. It seemed that a party was somehow able to bring into sharp focus something which in the blur of everyday life might easily escape. Under its glare and because of its stresses people became vulnerable. The novel *Mrs Dalloway,* published in 1925, focuses on such an occasion. Virginia Woolf had, however, to make its particular party spill over and beyond the actual novel itself. The party as such was larger than that party which formed the climax and central occasion of the novel. The novel comes to an end; the party goes on. Mrs Dalloway's party lives on after and beyond the novel in which it was created. The present volume is the book of that party.

So, besides the first draft version* which did take shape, the Mrs Dalloway stories also unexpectedly fell into place. Virginia Woolf published 'Mrs Dalloway in Bond Street' in *The Dial* in 1923. Leonard Woolf published four of the stories in *A Haunted House and Other Stories* in 1943. Two are being published now for the first time. It was the position of the stories

*Mrs Dalloway: A First Draft Version, should appear in 1973.

in the Berg MS that started the exploration that led to the present volume and to my conclusion that the stories belonged together as a group. It became possible, for example, to ascertain with a certain accuracy to what extent Virginia Woolf had been writing short stories concurrently with the writing of her novel. It seemed to me that the stories were conceived: either as parts of the novel itself, later to be rejected and to swim free as independent stories; or as alternative parallel expressions of Virginia Woolf's ideas.

It is particularly uncharacteristic of Virginia Woolf's normal writing habits that she should have allowed her completed novel's central concern to retain the hold on her imagination that it obviously then had. On finishing the.novel she wrote out several of the short stories about Mrs Dalloway's party. Usually when she had finally revised a novel, Virginia Woolf was only too anxious, as it were, to shut it out of her mind. This she did either by concentrating on a new novel, creating a different kind of novel, or by turning to writing of a non-fictional nature.

The seven stories in the present volume belong to the period between *Jacob's Room* (1922) and *To the Lighthouse* (1927). The novel of that period is *Mrs Dalloway*. The stories, as it were, surround that novel. It is not necessary to read the novel *Mrs Dalloway* in order to appreciate the book of short stories I have named *Mrs Dalloway's Party*. On the other hand, the book of short stories does enlarge one's understanding and appreciation of Virginia Woolf's work as a whole. It explains why, for example, the Mr and Mrs Dalloway who appear in *The Voyage Out* (1915) are still being written about in 1925. Virginia Woolf is not repeating herself; she is moving deeper into the Dalloway world, the society world, in order to fathom its power and question its values. The party created by Mrs Dalloway belongs to a particularly significant stage of Virginia Woolf's development as a novelist and a critic; it is significant biographically too.

Virginia Woolf loved society and its functions:

> The idea of a party always excited her, and in practice she was very sensitive to the actual mental and physical excitement of the party itself, the rise of temperature of mind and body, the ferment and fountain of noise.
>
> LEONARD WOOLF, *Downhill All the Way*

It was out of the excitement, the fluctuations of mood and temper, and the heightened atmosphere of the party that Virginia Woolf created the microcosm of society which she gives to us in her Mrs Dalloway stories.

But because of her severe bouts of illness in 1921 and 1922, the Woolfs had left London for the quiet of Richmond, though when Virginia was fit, they travelled to London to enjoy a limited social life. As her health improved in 1923 she began to feel imprisoned or cut off in Richmond and longed to return to the city, its noise and vitality. In early 1924 the Woolfs returned to London. The imposed restriction on her attendance at parties in the three years 1921 to 1923, and the return to a fuller enjoyment of society and its functions in 1924, seem to me to be reflected in her preoccupation with that world in the novel and the short stories written roughly within those years.

It was on 27th April 1925, when *Mrs Dalloway* was about to come out that Virginia Woolf made the following significant entry in her Diary:

But my present reflection is that people have any number of states of consciousness: and I should like to investigate the *party consciousness,* the frock consciousness etc. The fashion world of the Becks . . . is certainly one; where people secrete an envelope which connects them and protects them from others, like myself, who am outside the envelope, foreign bodies. These states are very difficult (obviously I grope for words) but I'm always coming back to it. The party consciousness. . . .

It seems that Virginia Woolf actually did make an investigation into the 'party consciousness' in her group of Mrs Dalloway short stories. It is the psychology of the party, the subtleties of the human being's reactions and anxieties under the conditions and limits imposed on him by the social occasion that are closely scrutinised by Virginia Woolf in *Mrs Dalloway's Party*. The artificiality of the occasion brings the reality to the fore or gives access to it. So, for example, Mabel Waring in 'The New Dress' reflects:

For the party makes things either much more real, or much less real, she thought. . . . She saw the truth. This was true, this drawing-room, this self, and the other false.

But for Mrs Vallance in 'Ancestors', on the other hand, the world of Mrs Dalloway's drawing-room is but a 'noisy bright chattering crowd' with which she contrasts the more worthwhile world of her childhood spent in the country, in Scotland. The two pieces, 'Introduction' and 'The Man Who Loved His Kind', both explore the solitary reflections of the individual alone in the midst of a group of men and women who are united only in that they are physically placed together in the drawing-room or home of Mrs Dalloway. The actual title 'Together and Apart' suggests what happens to two individuals at the party: Miss Anning and Mr Serle, introduced to each other by Mrs Dalloway, come together, or relate to each other, but only within the bounds of the party. They experience the 'old ecstasy of life' but their brief experience does not endure beyond the party or the story. There is, in other words, a brief 'coming together' which is resolved into a return to separateness or falling 'apart'. 'A Summing Up', the last story or chapter of *Mrs Dalloway's Party,* provides a key passage for an understanding of the short stories and of Virginia Woolf's 'party consciousness'. A tribute is paid to Clarissa Dalloway's creative ability. It is a bow to the hostess who is responsible for the occasion and the world she has created:

> This, she thought, is the greatest of marvels; the supreme achievement of the human race . . . and she thought of the dry, thick, well-built house, stored with valuables, humming with people coming close to each other, going away from each other, exchanging their views, stimulating each other. And Clarissa Dalloway had made it open in the wastes of the night. . . .

Yet the point of view of the story and of the actual summing up is complex like the party itself, for in a moment of disenchantment and detachment the person who made the bow to Mrs Dalloway asks herself if the party is after all nothing more than 'people in evening dress'.

Of the stories in the present volume 'Mrs Dalloway in Bond Street' is the one most closely connected with the genesis of the novel *Mrs Dalloway*. It was intended originally to be Chapter One of that novel. Although the story is obviously heavily echoed in the novel, it was rejected from the novel by Virginia Woolf who herself published it independently as a short story in 1923. 'The New Dress' was written in 1924 when Virginia Woolf was revising *Mrs Dalloway* for publication. In a pencil note to the manuscript opening of the story Virginia Woolf states:

> *The New Dress*
> At Mrs D's party
> She got it on this theory
> the theory of clothes
> but very little money
> this brings in the relation with
> sex; her estimate of herself.

'Mrs Dalloway in Bond Street' and 'The New Dress' are both connected with the genesis of the novel *Mrs Dalloway;* the other five stories written consecutively and probably not later than May 1925 form a kind of epilogue to it. Though the party goes on after the novel is finished Mrs Dalloway's is no longer its central consciousness. The focus now shifts from guest to guest revealing their reflections and insights. It is the other side of Mrs Dalloway's party. The seven stories or chapters, therefore, besides being all centred on Mrs Dalloway were also all written more or less at the same time as the novel.

The Mrs Dalloway stories, then, do form a related group in that they relate to each other thematically: the social theme and subject of the party and the actual or implied presence of Mrs

Dalloway give a unity to them. There is, too, a simple narrative and chronological unity to the 'stories'. At the narrative level the first two stories in the present collection anticipate the party: Mrs Dalloway is in Bond Street on the morning of the day on which she is to give her party. The Man Who Loved His Kind meets Mr Dalloway in Dean's Yard and is invited to drop in on the party. The remaining five 'chapters' are set at the party and the final chapter does in fact provide A Summing Up.

The new book which I have called *Mrs Dalloway's Party* does have a definite, though very simple, compositional form. The form it takes, or which I have given to it, was that intended originally for the novel *Mrs Dalloway*. That novel was first thought of as being possibly *At Home* or *The Party*. The Berg manuscript which contains Virginia Woolf's compositional notes for *Mrs Dalloway* has in it the following entry:

Oct. 6th 1922. Thoughts upon beginning a book to be called, perhaps, At Home: or The Party:

This is to be a short book consisting of six or seven chapters, each complete separately.
Yet there must be some sort of fusion!
And all must converge upon the party at the end.

This plan was abandoned by Virginia Woolf and the novel itself was altered radically in the course of its composition. But the plan fits perfectly the present volume of short stories. *Mrs Dalloway's Party* is a short book consisting of seven 'chapters', each complete separately and having, as I have tried to show, some sort of fusion, and all converging on or centring in the party.

Virginia Woolf's interest in the short story is something that can be traced back further than the sudden intense probing of the party and its world in 1925. By 1919 Virginia Woolf had proved herself to be a successful short story writer, particularly with the publication of *The Mark on the Wall*, and *Kew Gardens*. Or again, in experimenting with the form of the novel at the beginning of 1920 she finds her structural norm in the short story:

> Whether I'm sufficiently mistress of things – that's the doubt; but conceive [?] *Mark on the Wall, K.G.* and *Unwritten Novel* taking hands and dancing in unity. What the unity shall be I have yet to discover; the theme is a blank to me; but I see immense possibilities in the form I hit upon more or less by chance two weeks ago. . . .
>
> *(A Writer's Diary, p. 23)*

With the completion of *Mrs Dalloway* at the end of 1924 Virginia Woolf with almost a sense of release, turns again, only with greater concentration, to the short story proper:

> – and then I shall be free. Free at least to write out one or two more stories which have accumulated. I am less and less sure that they are stories, or what they are. Only I do feel fairly sure that I am grazing as near as I can to my own ideas, and getting a tolerable shape for them.
>
> *(A Writer's Diary, p. 70)*

On 19th April 1925, Virginia Woolf states that she wants to 'dig deep down' into her short stories. Then suddenly on the following day one learns that something has obviously happened, for she adds in her diary that she has now six stories 'welling up' in her. Then again, on May 14th, Virginia Woolf writes that before beginning work on her new novel (*To the Lighthouse*) she must 'write a few little stories first'. The 'few little stories' are contained in the present volume. Within roughly the first six months of 1925, therefore, two of Virginia Woolf's major literary preoccupations were the exploring of what she refers to as the 'party consciousness' and the writing of short 'stories', or small fictional fragments, of whose exact nature she was herself unsure. The two preoccupations interlock in that the 'stories' together explore a collected or varied party consciousness.

The seven 'chapters' of *Mrs Dalloway's Party* do not form an integral or organic whole comparable to the novel *Mrs Dalloway*, or indeed to any of Virginia Woolf's major novels, but the seven fictional pieces do fit together to form a kind of mosaic which has behind it the inner logic of a psychological exploration induced by the particular situation and occasion of the party.

Mrs Dalloway's Party

1

Mrs Dalloway in Bond Street

MRS DALLOWAY SAID she would buy the gloves herself. Big Ben was striking as she stepped out into the street. It was eleven o'clock and the unused hour was fresh as if issued to children on a beach. But there was something solemn in the deliberate swing of the repeated strokes; something stirring in the murmur of wheels and the shuffle of footsteps.

No doubt they were not all bound on errands of happiness. There is much more to be said about us than that we walk the streets of Westminster. Big Ben too is nothing but steel rods consumed by rust were it not for the care of H.M's Office of Works. Only for Mrs Dalloway the moment was complete; for Mrs Dalloway June was fresh. A happy childhood – and it was not to his daughters only that Justin Parry had seemed a fine fellow (weak of course on the Bench); flowers at evening, smoke rising; the caw of rooks falling from ever so high, down down through the October air – there is nothing to take the place of childhood. A leaf of mint brings it back: or a cup with a blue ring.

Poor little wretches, she sighed, and pressed forward. Oh, right under the horses' noses, you little demon! and there she was left on the kerb stretching her hand out, while Jimmy Dawes grinned on the further side.

A charming woman, posed, eager, strangely white-haired for her pink cheeks, so Scope Purvis, C.B., saw her as he hurried to his office. She stiffened a little, waiting for Durtnall's van to pass. Big Ben struck the tenth; struck the eleventh stroke. The leaden circles dissolved in the air. Pride held her erect, inheriting, handing on, acquainted with discipline and with suffering. How people suffered, how they suffered, she thought, thinking of Mrs Foxcroft at the Embassy last night decked with jewels, eating her heart out, because that nice boy was dead, and now the old Manor House (Durtnall's van passed) must go to a cousin.

'Good morning to you,' said Hugh Whitbread raising his hat rather extravagantly by the china shop, for they had known each other as children. 'Where are you off to?'

'I love walking in London,' said Mrs Dalloway. 'Really it's better than walking in the country!'

'We've just come up,' said Hugh Whitbread. 'Unfortunately to see doctors.'

'Milly?' said Mrs Dalloway, instantly compassionate.

'Out of sorts,' said Hugh Whitbread. 'That sort of thing. Dick all right?'

'First rate!' said Clarissa.

Of course, she thought, walking on, Milly is about my age – fifty – fifty-two. So it is probably *that*. Hugh's manner had said so, said it perfectly – dear old Hugh, thought Mrs Dalloway, remembering with amusement, with gratitude, with emotion, how shy, like a brother – one would rather die than speak to one's brother – Hugh had always been, when he was at Oxford, and came over, and perhaps one of them (drat the thing!) couldn't ride. How then could women sit in Parliament? How could they do things with men? For there is this extraordinarily deep instinct, something inside one; you can't get over it; it's no use trying; and men like Hugh respect it without our saying it, which is what one loves, thought Clarissa, in dear old Hugh.

She had passed through the Admiralty Arch and saw at the end of the empty road with its thin trees Victoria's white mound, Victoria's billowing motherliness, amplitude and homeliness, always ridiculous, yet how sublime thought Mrs Dalloway, remembering Kensington Gardens and the old lady in horn spectacles and being told by Nanny to stop dead still and bow to the Queen. The flag flew above the Palace. The King and Queen were back then. Dick had met her at lunch the other day – a thoroughly nice woman. It matters so much to the poor, thought Clarissa, and to the soldiers. A man in bronze stood heroically on a pedestal with a gun on her left hand side – the South African war. It matters, thought Mrs Dalloway walking towards Buckingham Palace. There it stood four-square, in the broad sunshine, uncompromising, plain. But it was character she thought; something inborn in the race; what Indians respected. The Queen went to hospitals, opened bazaars – the Queen of England, thought Clarissa, looking at the Palace. Already at this hour a motor car passed out at the gates; soldiers saluted; the gates were shut. And Clarissa, crossing the road, entered the Park, holding herself upright.

June had drawn out every leaf on the trees. The mothers of Westminster with mottled breasts gave suck to their young. Quite respectable girls lay stretched on the grass. An elderly man, stooping very stiffly, picked up a crumpled paper, spread it out flat and flung it away. How horrible! Last night at the Embassy Sir Dighton had said, 'If I want a fellow to hold my horse, I have only to put up my hand.' But the religious question is far more serious than the economic, Sir Dighton had said, which she thought extraordinarily interesting, from a man like Sir Dighton. 'Oh, the country will never know what it has lost,' he had said, talking, of his own accord, about dear Jack Stewart.

She mounted the little hill lightly. The air stirred with energy. Messages were passing from the Fleet to the Admiralty. Piccadilly and Arlington Street and the Mall seemed to chafe the very air in the Park and lift its leaves hotly, brilliantly, upon waves of that divine vitality which Clarissa loved. To ride; to dance; she had adored all that. Or going long walks in the country, talking, about books, what to do with one's life, for young people were amazingly priggish – oh, the things one had said! But one had conviction. Middle age is the devil. People like Jack'll never know that, she thought; for he never once thought of death, never, they said, knew he was dying. And now can never mourn – how did it go? – a head grown grey. . . . From the contagion of the world's slow stain. . . . Have drunk their cup a round or two before. . . . From the contagion of the world's slow stain! She held herself upright.

But how Jack would have shouted! Quoting Shelley, in Piccadilly! 'You want a pin,' he would have said. He hated frumps. 'My God Clarissa! My God Clarissa!' – she could hear him now at the Devonshire House party, about poor Sylvia Hunt in her amber necklace and that dowdy old silk. Clarissa held herself upright for she had spoken aloud and now she was in Piccadilly, passing the house with the slender green columns, and the balconies; passing club windows full of newspapers; passing old Lady Burdett Coutt's house where the glazed white parrot used to hang; and Devonshire House, without its gilt leopards; and Claridge's, where she must remember Dick wanted her to leave a card on Mrs Jepson or she would be gone. Rich Americans can be very charming. There was St James's Palace; like a child's game with bricks; and now – she had passed Bond Street – she was by Hatchard's book shop. The stream was endless – endless – endless. Lords, Ascot, Hurlingham – what was it? What a duck, she thought, looking at the frontispiece of some book of memoirs spread wide in the bow window, Sir Joshua perhaps or Romney; arch, bright, demure; the sort of girl – like her own Elizabeth – the only *real* sort of girl. And there was that absurd book, *Soapy Sponge,* which Jum used to quote by the yard; and Shakespeare's Sonnets. She knew them by heart. Phil and she had argued all day about the Dark Lady, and Dick had said straight out at dinner that night that he had never heard of her. Really, she had married him for that! He had never read Shakespeare! There must be some little cheap book she could buy for Milly – *Cranford* of course! Was there ever anything so enchanting as the cow in petticoats? If only people had that sort of humour, that sort of self-respect now, thought Clarissa, for she remembered the broad pages; the sentences ending; the characters – how one talked about them as if they were real. For all the great things one must go to the past, she thought. From the contagion of the world's slow stain. . . . Fear no more the heat o' the sun. . . . And now can never mourn, can never mourn, she repeated, her eyes straying over the window; for it

7

ran in her head; the test of great poetry; the moderns had never written anything one wanted to read about death, she thought; and turned.

Omnibuses joined motor cars; motor cars vans; vans taxicabs; taxicabs motor cars – here was an open motor car with a girl, alone. Up till four, her feet tingling, I know, thought Clarissa, for the girl looked washed out, half asleep, in the corner of the car after the dance. And another car came; and another. No! No! No! Clarissa smiled good-naturedly. The fat lady had taken every sort of trouble, but diamonds! orchids! at this hour of the morning! No! No! No! The excellent policeman would, when the time came, hold up his hand. Another motor car passed. How utterly unattractive! Why should a girl of that age paint black round her eyes? And a young man with a girl, at this hour, when the country – The admirable policeman raised his hand and Clarissa acknowledging his sway, taking her time, crossed, walked towards Bond Street; saw the narrow crooked street, the yellow banners; the thick notched telegraph wires stretched across the sky.

A hundred years ago her great-great-grandfather, Seymour Parry, who ran away with Conway's daughter, had walked down Bond Street. Down Bond Street the Parrys had walked for a hundred years, and might have met the Dalloways (Leighs on the mother's side) going up. Her father got his clothes from Hill's. There was a roll of cloth in the window, and here just one jar on a black table, incredibly expensive; like the thick pink salmon on the ice block at the fishmonger's. The jewels were exquisite – pink and orange stars, paste, Spanish, she thought, and chains of old gold; starry buckles, little brooches which had been worn on sea-green satin by ladies with high head-dresses. But no looking! One must economise. She must go on past the picture dealer's where one of the odd French pictures hung, as if people had thrown confetti – pink and blue – for a joke. If you had lived with pictures (and it's the same with books and music) thought Clarissa, passing the Aeolian Hall, you can't be taken in by a joke.

The river of Bond Street was clogged. There, like a queen at a tournament, raised, regal, was Lady Bexborough. She sat in her carriage, upright, alone, looking through her glasses. The white glove was loose at her wrist. She was in black, quite shabby, yet, thought Clarissa, how extraordinarily it tells, breeding, self-respect, never saying a word too much or letting people gossip; an astonishing friend; no one can pick a hole in her after all these years, and now, there she is, thought Clarissa, passing the Countess who waited powdered, perfectly still, and Clarissa would have given anything to be like that, the mistress of Clarefield, talking politics, like a man. But she never goes anywhere, thought Clarissa, and it's quite useless to ask her, and the carriage went on and Lady Bexborough was borne past like a queen at a tournament, though she had nothing to live for and the old man is failing and they say she is sick of it all, thought Clarissa and the tears actually rose to her eyes as she entered the shop.

'Good morning,' said Clarissa in her charming voice. 'Gloves,' she said with her exquisite friendliness and putting her bag on the counter began, very slowly, to undo the buttons. 'White gloves', she said. 'Above the elbow,' and she looked straight into the shop-woman's face – but this was not the girl she remembered? She looked quite old. 'These really don't fit,' said Clarissa. The shop-girl looked at them.

'Madame wears bracelets?' Clarissa spread out her fingers. 'Perhaps it's my rings,' And the girl took the grey gloves with her to the end of the counter.

Yes, thought Clarissa, it's the girl I remember, she's twenty years older. . . . There was only one other customer, sitting sideways at the counter, her elbow poised, her bare hand drooping vacant; like a figure on a Japanese fan, thought Clarissa, too vacant perhaps, yet some men would adore her. The lady shook her head sadly. Again the gloves were too large. She turned round the glass. 'Above the wrist,' she reproached the grey-headed woman, who looked and agreed.

They waited; a clock ticked; Bond Street hummed, dulled, distant; the woman went away holding gloves. 'Above the wrist,' said the lady, mournfully, raising her voice. And she would have to order chairs, ices, flowers, and cloak-room tickets, thought Clarissa. The people she didn't want would come; the others wouldn't. She would stand by the door. They sold stockings – silk stockings. A lady is known by her gloves and her shoes, old Uncle William used to say. And through the hanging silk stockings, quivering silver she looked at the lady, sloping shouldered, her hand drooping, her bag slipping, her eyes vacantly on the floor. It would be intolerable if dowdy women came to her party! Would one have liked Keats if he had worn red socks? Oh, at last – she drew into the counter and it flashed into her mind:

'Do you remember before the war you had gloves with pearl buttons?'

'French gloves, Madame?'

'Yes, they were French,' said Clarissa. The other lady rose very sadly and took her bag, and looked at the gloves on the counter. But they were all too large – always too large at the wrist.

'With pearl buttons,' said the shop-girl, who looked ever so much older. She split the lengths of tissue paper apart on the counter. With pearl buttons, thought Clarissa, perfectly simple – how French!

'Madame's hands are so slender,' said the shop-girl, drawing the glove firmly, smoothly, down over her rings. And Clarissa looked at her arm in the looking-glass. The glove hardly came to the elbow. Were there others half an inch longer? Still it seemed tiresome to bother her – perhaps the one day in the month, thought Clarissa, when it's an agony to stand. 'Oh, don't bother,' she said. But the gloves were brought.

'Don't you get fearfully tired,' she said in her charming voice, 'standing? When d'you get your holiday?'

'In September, Madame, when we're not so busy.'

When we're in the country thought Clarissa. Or shooting. She has a fortnight at Brighton. In some stuffy lodging. The landlady takes the sugar. Nothing would be easier than to send her to Mrs Lumley's right in the country (and it was on the tip of her tongue). But then she remembered how on their honeymoon Dick had shown her the folly of giving impulsively. It was much more important, he said, to get trade with China. Of course he was right. And she could feel the girl wouldn't like to be given things. There she was in her place. So was Dick. Selling gloves was her job. She had her own sorrows quite separate, 'and now can never mourn, can never mourn', the words ran in her head, 'From the contagion of the world's slow stain,' thought Clarissa holding her arm stiff, for there are moments when it seems utterly futile (the glove was drawn off leaving her arm flecked with powder) – simply one doesn't believe, thought Clarissa, any more in God.

The traffic suddenly roared; the silk stockings brightened. A customer came in.

'White gloves,' she said, with some ring in her voice that Clarissa remembered.

It used, thought Clarissa, to be so simple. Down, down through the air came the caw of the rooks. When Sylvia died, hundreds of years ago, the yew hedges looked so lovely with the diamond webs in the mist before early church. But if Dick were to die to-morrow? As for believing in God – no, she would let the children choose, but for herself, like Lady Bexborough, who opened the bazaar, they say, with the telegram in her hand – Roden, her favourite, killed – she would go on. But why, if one doesn't believe? For the sake of others, she thought taking the glove in her hand. The girl would be much more unhappy if she didn't believe.

'Thirty shillings,' said the shop-woman. 'No, pardon me Madame, thirty-five. The French gloves are more.'

For one doesn't live for oneself, thought Clarissa.

And then the other customer took a glove, tugged it, and it split.

'There!' she exclaimed.

'A fault of the skin,' said the grey-headed woman hurriedly. 'Sometimes a drop of acid in tanning. Try this pair, Madame.'

'But it's an awful swindle to ask two pound ten!'

Clarissa looked at the lady; the lady looked at Clarissa.

'Gloves have never been quite so reliable since the war,' said the shop-girl, apologising, to Clarissa.

But where had she seen the other lady? – elderly, with a frill under her chin; wearing a black ribbon for gold eyeglasses; sensual, clever, like a Sargent drawing. How one can tell from a voice when people are in the habit, thought Clarissa, of making other people – 'It's a shade too tight,' she said – obey. The shop-woman went off again. Clarissa was left waiting. Fear no more she repeated, playing her finger on the counter. Fear no more the heat o' the sun. Fear no more she repeated. There were little brown spots on her arm. And the girl crawled like a snail. Thou thy worldly task hast done. Thousands of young men had died that things might go on. At last! Half an inch above the elbow; pearl buttons; five and a quarter. My dear slowcoach, thought Clarissa, do you think I can sit here the whole morning? Now you'll take twenty-five minutes to bring me my change!

There was a violent explosion in the street outside. The shop-women cowered behind the counters. But Clarissa, sitting very upright, smiled at the other lady. 'Miss Anstruther!' she exclaimed.

2

The Man Who Loved His Kind

TROTTING THROUGH DEANS Yard that afternoon, Prickett Ellis ran straight into Richard Dalloway, or rather, just as they were passing, the covert side glance which each was casting on the other, under his hat, over his shoulder, broadened and burst into recognition; they had not met for twenty years. They had been at school together. And what was Ellis doing? The Bar? Of course, of course – he had followed the case in the papers. But it was impossible to talk here. Wouldn't he drop in that evening. (They lived in the same old place – just round the corner.) One or two people were coming. Joynson perhaps. 'An awful swell now,' said Richard.

'Good – till this evening then,' said Richard, and went his way, 'jolly glad' (that was quite true) to have met that queer chap, who hadn't changed one bit since he had been at school – just the same knobbly, chubby little boy then, with prejudices sticking out all over him, but uncommonly brilliant – won the Newcastle. Well – off he went.

Prickett Ellis, however, as he turned and looked at Dalloway disappearing, wished how he had not met him or, at least, for he had always liked him personally, hadn't promised to come to this party. Dalloway was married, gave parties; wasn't his sort at all. He would have to dress. However, as the evening drew on, he supposed, as he had said that, and didn't want to be rude, he must go there.

But what an appalling entertainment! There was Joynson; they had nothing to say to each other. He had been a pompous little boy; he had grown rather more self-important – that was all; there wasn't a single other soul in the room that Prickett Ellis knew. Not one. So, as he could not go at once, without saying a word to Dalloway, who seemed altogether taken up with his duties, bustling about in a white waistcoat, there he had to stand. It was the sort of thing that made his gorge rise. Think of a grown-up, responsible men and women doing this every night of their lives! The lines deepened on his blue and red shaven cheeks as he leant against the wall in complete silence, for though he worked like a horse, he kept himself fit by exercise; and he looked hard and fierce, as if his moustaches were dipped in frost. He bristled; he grated. His meagre dress clothes made him look unkempt, insignificant, angular.

Idle, chattering, overdressed, without an idea in their heads, these fine ladies and gentlemen went on talking and laughing; and Prickett Ellis watched them and compared them with the Brunners who, when they won their case against Fenners' Brewery and got two hundred pounds compensation (it was not half what they should have got) went and spent five of it on a clock for him. That was a decent sort of thing to do; that was the sort of thing that moved one, and he glared more severely than ever at these people, overdressed, cynical, prosperous, and compared what he felt now with what he felt at

15

eleven o'clock that morning when old Brunner and Mrs Brunner, in their best clothes, awfully respectable and clean looking old people, had called in to give him that small token, as the old man put it, standing perfectly upright to make his speech of gratitude and respect for the very able way in which you conducted our case, and Mrs Brunner piped up, how it was all due to him they felt. And they deeply appreciated his generosity – because, of course, he hadn't taken a fee.

And as he took the clock and put it on the middle of his mantelpiece, he had felt that he wished nobody to see his face. That was what he worked for – that was his reward; and he looked at the people who were actually before his eyes as if they danced over the scene in his chambers and were exposed by it, and as it faded – the Brunners faded – there remained as if left of that scene, himself, confronting this hostile population, a perfectly plain unsophisticated man, a man of the people (he straightened himself), very badly dressed, glaring, with not an air or a grace about him, a man who was an ill hand at concealing his feelings, a plain man, an ordinary human being, pitted against the evil, the corruption, the heartlessness of society. But he would not go on staring. Now he put on his spectacles and examined the pictures. He read the titles on a line of books; for the most part poetry. He would have liked well enough to read some of his old favourites again – Shakespeare, Dickens – he wished he ever had time to turn into the National Gallery, but he couldn't – no, one could not. Really one could not – with the world in the state it was in. Not when people all day long wanted your help, fairly clamoured for help. This wasn't an age for luxuries. And he looked at the armchairs and the paper-knives and the well-bound books, and shook his head, knowing that he would never have the time, never, he was glad to think, have the heart, to afford himself such luxuries. The people here would be shocked if they knew what he paid for his tobacco; how he had borrowed his clothes. His one and only extravagance was his little yacht on the Norfolk Broads. And that he did allow himself. He did like once a year to get right away from every-body and lie once a year on his back in a field. He thought how shocked they would be – these fine folk – if they realised the amount of pleasure he got from what he was old-fashioned enough to call the love of nature; trees and fields he had known ever since he was a boy.

These fine people would be shocked. Indeed, standing there, putting his spectacles away in his pocket, he felt himself grow more and more shocking every instant. And it was a very disagreeable feeling. He did not feel this – that he loved humanity, that he paid only fivepence an ounce for tobacco and loved nature – naturally and quietly. Each of these pleasures had been turned into a protest. He felt that these people whom he despised made him stand and deliver and justify himself. 'I am an ordinary man,' he kept saying. And what he said next he was really ashamed of saying, but he said it. 'I have done more for my kind in one day than the rest of you in all your lives.' Indeed, he could not help himself; he kept recalling scene after scene, like that when the Brunners gave him the clock – he kept reminding himself of the nice things people had said of his humanity, of his generosity, how he had helped them. He kept seeing himself as the wise and tolerant servant of humanity. And he wished he could repeat his praises aloud. It was unpleasant that the sense of his goodness should boil within him. It was still more unpleasant that he could tell no one what people had said about him. Thank the Lord, he kept saying, I shall be back at work to-morrow; and yet he was no longer satisfied simply to slip through the door and go home. He must stay, he must stay until he had justified himself. But how could he? In all that room full of people, he did not know a soul to speak to.

At last Richard Dalloway came up.

'I want to introduce Miss O'Keefe,' he said. Miss O'Keefe looked him full in the eyes. She was a rather arrogant, abrupt-mannered woman in the thirties.

Miss O'Keefe wanted an ice or something to drink. And the reason why she asked Prickett Ellis to give it her in what he felt a haughty, unjustifiable manner, was that she had seen a woman and two children, very poor, very tired, pressing against the railings of a square, peering in, that hot afternoon. Can't they be let in? she had thought, her pity rising like a wave; her indignation boiling. No; she rebuked herself the next moment, roughly, as if she boxed her own ears. The whole force of the world can't do it. So she picked up the tennis ball and hurled it back. The whole force of the world can't do it, she said in a fury, and that was why she said so commandingly, to the unknown man:

'Give me an ice.'

Long before she had eaten it, Prickett Ellis, standing beside her without taking anything, told her that he had not been to a party for fifteen years; told her that his dress suit was lent him by his brother-in-law; told her that he did not like this sort of thing, and it would have eased him greatly to go on to say that he was a plain man, who happened to have a liking for ordinary people, and then would have told her (and been ashamed of it afterwards) about the Brunners and the clock, but she said:

'Have you seen the *Tempest*?'

then (for he had not seen the *Tempest*), had he read some book? Again no, and then, putting her ice down, did he ever read poetry?

And Prickett Ellis feeling something rise within him which would decapitate this young woman, make a victim of her, massacre her, made her sit down there, where they would not be interrupted, on two chairs, in the empty garden, for everyone was upstairs, only you could hear a buzz and a hum and a chatter and a jingle, like the mad accompaniment of some phantom orchestra to a cat or two slinking across the grass, and the wavering of leaves, and the yellow and red fruit like Chinese lanterns wobbling this way and that – the talk seemed like a frantic skeleton dance music set to something very real, and full of suffering.

'How beautiful!' said Miss O'Keefe.

Oh, it was beautiful, this little patch of grass, with the towers of Westminster massed round it black, high in the air, after the drawing-room; it was silent, after that noise. After all, they had that – the tired woman, the children.

Prickett Ellis lit a pipe. That would shock her; he filled it with shag tobacco – fivepence-halfpenny an ounce. He thought how he would lie in his boat smoking, he could see himself, alone, at night, smoking under the stars. For always to-night he kept thinking how he would look if these people here were to see him. He said to Miss O'Keefe, striking a match on the sole of his boot, that he couldn't see anything particularly beautiful out here.

19

'Perhaps,' said Miss O'Keefe, 'you don't care for beauty.' (He had told her that he had not seen the *Tempest;* that he had not read a book; he looked ill-kempt, all moustached, chin, and silver watch chain.) She thought nobody need pay a penny for this; the Museums are free and the National Gallery; and the country. Of course she knew the objections – the washing, cooking, children; but the root of things, what they were all afraid of saying, was that happiness is dirt cheap. You can have it for nothing. Beauty.

Then Prickett Ellis let her have it – this pale, abrupt, arrogant woman. He told her, puffing his shag tobacco, what he had done that day. Up at six; interviews; smelling a drain in a filthy slum; then to court.

Here he hesitated, wishing to tell her something of his own doings. Suppressing that, he was all the more caustic. He said it made him sick to hear well-fed, well-dressed women (she twitched her lips, for she was thin, and her dress not up to standard) talk of beauty.

'Beauty!' he said. He was afraid he did not understand beauty apart from human beings.

So they glared into the empty garden where the lights were swaying, and one cat hesitating in the middle, its paw lifted.

Beauty apart from human beings? What did he mean by that? she demanded suddenly.

Well this; getting more and more wrought up, he told her the story of the Brunners and the clock, not concealing his pride in it. That was beautiful, he said.

She had no words to specify the horror his story roused in her. First his conceit; then his indecency in talking about human feelings; it was a blasphemy; no one in the whole world

20

ought to tell a story to prove that they had loved their kind. Yet as he told it – how the old man had stood up and made his speech – tears came into her eyes; ah, if any one had ever said that to her! but then again, she felt how it was just this that condemned humanity for ever; never would they reach beyond affecting scenes with clocks; Brunners making speeches to Prickett Ellises, and the Prickett Ellises would always say how they had loved their kind; they would always be lazy, compromising, and afraid of beauty. Hence sprang revolutions; from laziness and fear and this love of affecting scenes. Still this man got pleasure from his Brunners; and she was condemned to suffer for ever and ever from her poor, poor women shut out from squares. So they sat silent. Both were very unhappy. For Prickett Ellis was not in the least solaced by what he had said; instead of picking her thorn out he had rubbed it in; his happiness of the morning had been ruined. Miss O'Keefe was muddled and annoyed; she was muddy instead of clear.

'I am afraid I am one of those very ordinary people,' he said, getting up, 'who love their kind.'

Upon which Miss O'Keefe almost shouted: 'So do I.'

Hating each other, hating the whole houseful of people who had given them this painful, this disillusioning evening, these two lovers of their kind got up, and without a word, parted for ever.

3

The Introduction

LILY EVERIT SAW Mrs Dalloway bearing down on her from the other side of the room, and could have prayed her not to come and disturb her; and yet, as Mrs Dalloway approached with her right hand raised and a smile which Lily knew (though this was her first party) meant: 'But you've got to come out of your corner and talk,' a smile at once benevolent and drastic, she felt the strangest mixture of excitement and fear, of desire to be left alone and of longing to be taken out and thrown into the boiling depths. But Mrs Dalloway was intercepted, caught by an old gentleman with white moustaches. So Lily Everit had two minutes respite there in which to hug to herself, as a drowning man might hug a spar in the sea, her essay on the character of Dean Swift. It had been given back to her that morning by Professor Miller marked with three red stars: First rate. First rate; she repeated that to herself, she took a sip of that cordial that was ever so much weaker now than it had been when she stood before the long glass being finished off (a pat here, a dab there) by her sister and Mildred, the housemaid. For as their hands moved about her she felt that they were fidgeting agreeably on the surface but beneath lay untouched like a lump of glowing metal – her essay on the character of Dean Swift, and all their praises when she came downstairs and stood in the hall waiting for the cab – Rupert had come out of his room and said what a swell she looked – ruffled the surface like a breeze among ribbons; but no more. Essays were the facts of life.

One divided life (she felt sure of it) into fact and into fiction, into rock and into wave, she thought, driving along and seeing things with such intensity that for ever and ever she would see the driver's back through the glass, and her own white phantom reflected in his dark coat. Then as she came into the house, at the very first sight of people moving upstairs and downstairs, this hard lump (her essay on the character of Swift) wobbled began wilting, she could not keep hold of it, and all her being (no longer sharp as a diamond cleaving the heart of life asunder) turned to a mist of alarm, apprehension, and defence, as she stood at bay in her corner. This was the famous place: the world.

Looking out, Lily Everit instinctively hid that essay of hers, so ashamed was she now, so bewildered too. And on tiptoe, nevertheless, to adjust her focus and get into right proportions (the old had been shamefully wrong) these diminishing and increasing things (what could one call them? people – impressions of people's lives?) which seemed to menace and mount over her, to turn everything to water, leaving her only the power to stand at bay.

Now Mrs Dalloway, who had never quite dropped her arm, had shown by the way she moved it that she was coming, left the old soldier with the white moustaches, and came straight

23

down on her, and said to the shy charming girl, with the clear eyes, the dark hair which clustered poetically round her head and the thin body in a dress which seemed to be slipping off, 'Come and let me introduce you,' and there Mrs Dalloway hesitated, and then remembering that Lily was the clever one who read poetry, looked about for some young man, some young man just down from Oxford, who would have read everything and would talk about himself. And holding Lily Everit's hand she led her towards a group where there were young people talking.

Lily Everit hung back a little, might have been in the wake of a steamer; felt as Mrs Dalloway led her on, that it was now going to happen; that nothing could prevent it, or save her (and she only wanted it to be over now) from being flung into a whirlpool where either she would perish or be saved. But what was the whirlpool?

Oh it was made of a million things and each so distinct to her; Westminster Abbey; the sense of enormously high solemn buildings surrounding them; grown up; being a woman. Perhaps that was the thing that came out, that remained, it was part of the dress, and all the little chivalries and respects of the drawing-room; all made her feel that she had come out of her chrysalis and was being proclaimed what in the long comfortable darkness of childhood she had never been – this frail and beautiful creature, this limited and circumscribed creature who could not do what she liked, this butterfly with a thousand facets to its eyes, and delicate fine plumage, and difficulties and sensibilities and sadnesses innumerable: a woman.

As she walked with Mrs Dalloway across the room she accepted the part which was now laid on her, and, naturally, overdid it a little, as a soldier proud of the traditions of an old and famous uniform might overdo it, feeling conscious as she walked of her finery; of her tight shoes; of her coiled and twisted hair; and how if she dropped a handkerchief (this had happened with strangers) a man would stoop precipitately and give it to her; thus accentuating the delicacy, the artificiality of her bearing unnaturally, for they were not hers after all.

Hers it was, rather, to run and hurry and ponder on long solitary walks, climbing gates, stepping through the mud, and through the blur, the dream, the ecstasy of loneliness, to see in the plover's wheel and surprise the rabbits, and come in the hearts of woods or wide lonely moors upon little ceremonies which had no audience, private rites, pure beauty offered by beetles and lilies of the valley and dead leaves and still pools, without any care whatever what human beings thought of them, which filled her mind with rapture and wonder – all this was, until tonight, her ordinary being, by which she knew and liked herself and crept into the heart of mother and father and brothers and sisters; and this other was a flower which had opened in ten minutes. And with the flower opened there came too, incontrovertibly, its world, so different, so strange; the towers of Westminster; the high and formal buildings; the talk; this civilisation, she felt, hanging back, as Mrs Dalloway led her on.

This regulated way of life which fell like a yoke about her neck, softly, indomitably, from the skies, a statement which there was no gainsaying. Glancing at her essay; the three red stars dulled to obscurity, but peacefully, pensively, as if yielding to the pressure of unquestionable might, that is the conviction that it was not hers to dominate, or to assert; rather to air and embellish this orderly life where all was done already; high towers, solemn bells, flats built every brick of them by men's toil, parliaments too; and even the criss-cross of telegraph wires she thought looking at the window as she walked. What had she to oppose to this massive masculine achievement? An essay on the character of Dean Swift! And as she came to the group, which Bob Brinsley dominated (with his heel on the fender, and his head back), with his great honest forehead, and his look of self-assurance, and his delicacy, and honour and robust physical well being, and sunburn, and airiness and direct descent from Shakespeare, what could she do but lay her essay, oh and the whole of her being, on the floor as a cloak for him to trample on, as a rose for him to rifle. Which she did, emphatically, when Mrs Dalloway said, still holding her hand as if she would run away from this supreme trial, this introduction, 'Mr Brinsley – Miss Everit'. Both of you love Shelley. But hers was not love compared with his.

Saying this, Mrs Dalloway felt, as she always felt remembering her youth, absurdly moved; youth meeting youth at her party, and there flashing, as at the concussion of steel upon flint (both stiffened to her feeling perceptibly) the loveliest and most ancient of all fires as she saw in Bob Brinsley's change of expression from carelessness to conformity, to formality, as he shook hands, which foreboded Clarissa thought, the tenderness, the goodness, the carelessness of women latent in all men, to her a sight to bring tears to the eyes, as it moved her even more intimately, to see in Lily herself the shy look, the startled look, surely the loveliest of all looks on a girl's face; and man feeling this for woman, and woman that for man, and there flowing from that contact all those homes, trials, sorrows, profound joy and intimate staunchness in the face of catastrophe, humanity was sweet at its heart, thought Clarissa, and her own life (to introduce a couple made her think of meeting Richard for the first time!) infinitely blessed. And on she went.

But, thought Lily Everit. But – But – But what?

Oh nothing, she thought hastily smothering down softly her sharp instinct. In the direct line from Shakespeare she thought and parliaments and churches she thought, oh and the telegraph wires too she thought, and ostentatiously of set purpose begged Mr Brinsley to believe her implicitly when she offered him her essay upon the character of Dean Swift to do what he liked with, trample upon and destroy, for how could a mere child understand even for an instant the character of Dean Swift. Yes, she said. She did like reading.

'And I suppose you write?' he said, 'poems presumably?'

'Essays,' she said. And she would not let this horror get possession of her. She wanted to have her handkerchief picked up on the staircase and be a butterfly. Churches and parliaments, flats, even the telegraph wires – all, she told herself, made by men of toil, and this young man, she told herself, in direct descent from Shakespeare, so she would not let this terror, this suspicion of something different, get hold of her and shrivel up her wings and drive her out into loneliness. But as she said this, she saw him – how else could she describe it – kill a fly. That was it. He tore the wings off a fly, standing with his foot on the fender his head thrown back, talking insolently about himself, arrogantly. But she didn't mind how insolent and arrogant he was to her, if only he had not been brutal to flies.

But she said, fidgeting as she smothered down that idea, why not, since he is the greatest of all worldly objects? And to worship, to adorn, to embellish was her task, her wings were for that. But he talked; but he looked; but he laughed; he tore the wings off a fly. He pulled the wings off its back with his clever strong hands, and she saw him do it and she could not hide the knowledge from herself. But it is necessary that it should be so, she argued, thinking of the churches, of the parliaments and the blocks of flats, and so tried to crouch and cower and fold the wings down flat on her back.

But – but, what was it, why was it? In spite of all she could do her essay upon the character of Swift became more and more obtrusive and the three stars burnt quite bright again, only with a terrible lustre, no longer clear and brilliant, but troubled and bloodstained, as if this man, this great Mr Brinsley, had just by pulling the wings off a fly as he talked (about his essays, about himself and once laughing, about a girl there) charged her light being with cloud, and confused her for ever and ever and shrivelled her wings on her back, and, as he turned away from her, she went nearer to the window and thought of the towers and civilisation with horror, and the yoke that had fallen from the skies onto her neck crushed her, and she felt like a naked wretch who having sought shelter in some shady garden is turned out and made to understand (ah, but there was a kind of passion in it too) that there are no sanctuaries, or butterflies, and this civilisation, said Lily Everit to herself, as she accepted the kind compliments of old Mrs Bromley on her appearance, depends upon me. Mrs Bromley said later that like all the Everits, Lily looked 'as if she had the weight of the world upon her shoulders'.

4

Ancestors

MRS VALLANCE, AS she replied to Jack Renshaw who had made that rather silly remark of his about not liking to watch cricket matches, wished that she could make him understand somehow what became every moment more obvious at a party like this, that if her father had been alive people would have realised how foolish, how wicked – no, not so much wicked as silly and ugly – how, compared to really dignified simple men and women like her father, like her dear mother, all this seemed to her so trivial. How very different his mind was, and his life; and her mother, and how differently, entirely differently she herself had been brought up.

'Here we all are,' she said suddenly, 'cooped up here in one room the size of an oven, when up in Scotland where I was born we should all be – ': she owed it to these foolish young men who were after all quite nice, though a little under-sized, to make them understand what her father, what her mother and she herself too, for she was like them at heart, felt. And then it came over her in a rush, how she owed it to the world to make men understand how her father and her mother, how she too, were quite different.

He had stopped in Edinburgh for a night once, Mr Renshaw said.

'Was she Scotch?' he asked.

He did not know then who her father was, that she was John Ellis Rattray's daughter and her mother was Catherine Macdonald; and one night in Edinburgh! And she had spent all those wonderful years there, there and at Elliotshaw on the Northumbrian border. There she had run wild among the currant bushes; there her father's friends had come and only a girl as she was, she had heard the most wonderful talk of her time. She could see them still; her father, Sir Duncan Clements, Mr Rogers (old Mr Rogers was her ideal of a Greek sage) sitting under the cedar tree; after dinner in the starlight.

They talked about everything in the world, it seemed to her now; they were too large-minded ever to laugh at other people; they had taught her, though she was only a girl, how to revere beauty. What was there beautiful in this stuffy London room?

'Oh, those poor flowers,' she exclaimed. For a carnation or two were actually trodden under foot, for petals of flowers were all crumpled and crushed. For she felt almost too much for flowers. Her mother had loved flowers; ever since she was a child she had been brought up to feel that to hurt a flower was to hurt the most exquisite thing in nature. Nature had always been a passion with her; the mountains, the sea. And here in London, one looked out of the window and saw more houses. One had a dreadful sense of human beings packed on top of each other in little boxes. It was an atmosphere in which she could not possibly live; herself; now she could not bear to walk in London and see the children in the streets. She was perhaps too sensitive; life would be impossible if everyone was like her, but when she remembered her own childhood, and her father and mother, and the beauty and care that were lavished on them –

'What a lovely frock!' said Jack Renshaw. And that seemed to her altogether wrong – for a young man to be noticing women's clothes at all. Her father was full of reverence for women, but he never thought of noticing what they wore. And of all these girls – the girls might be pretty – there was not a single one of them one could call beautiful as she remembered her mother, her dear stately mother who never seemed to dress differently summer or winter, whether they had people or not, but always looked herself in some lace and a black dress or, as she grew older, a little cap. When she was a widow she would sit among her flowers by the hour, and she seemed to be more with ghosts than with them all, dreaming of the past which is, Mrs Vallance thought, somehow so much more real than the present. But why!

It is in the past with those wonderful men and women, she thought, that I really live; it is they who knew me; it is those people only (and she thought of the starlit garden and the trees and old Mr Rogers, and her father, in his white linen coat, smoking) who understood me. She felt her eyes soften and deepen as at the approach of tears, standing there in Mrs Dalloway's drawing-room, looking at these people, these flowers, this noisy bright chattering crowd; at herself, that little girl who was to travel so far, running picking Sweet Alice, then sitting up in bed in the attic which smelt of pine-wood reading

31

stories, poetry. She had read all Shelley between the age of twelve and fifteen, and used to say it to her father, holding her hands behind her back, while he stared. The tears began, down in the back of her head, to rise, as she looked at this picture of herself, and added the suffering of a lifetime (she had suffered abominably, life had passed over her like a wheel, life was not what it had seemed then – it was like this party) to the child standing there, reciting Shelley, with her dark wild eyes. But what had they not seen later.

And it was only those people, dead now, laid away in quiet Scotland, who had ever seen all that she had it in her to be; who had known her, who knew what she had it in her to be. And now the tears came closer, as she thought of the little girl in the cotton frock; how large and dark her eyes were; how beautiful she looked repeating the 'Ode to the West Wind'; how proud her father was of her, and how great he was, and how great her mother even, and how when she was with them she was entirely so pure, so good, so gifted that she had it in her to be anything; that if they had lived, and she had always been with them in the garden (which now appeared the only place where she had spent her whole childhood, and it was always starlit, and always summer, and they were always sitting out under the cedar tree smoking, and except that somehow her mother was dreaming alone, in her widow's cap, among her flowers; and how good and kind and respectful the old servants were, Andrews the gardener, Jersy the cook; and old Sultan the Newfoundland dog; and the vine, and the pond, and the pump; and) – Mrs Vallance looking very fierce and proud and satirical, compared her life with other people's lives – and if that life could have gone on for ever, then Mrs

Vallance felt none of this – and she looked at Jack Renshaw and the girl whose clothes he admired – could have had any existence, and she would have been oh perfectly happy, perfectly good, instead of which here she was forced to listen to a young man saying – and she laughed almost scornfully and yet tears were in her eyes – that he could not bear to watch cricket matches!

5

Together and Apart

MRS DALLOWAY INTRODUCED them, saying you will like him. The conversation began some minutes before anything was said, for both Mr Serle and Miss Anning looked at the sky and in both of their minds the sky went on pouring its meaning, though very differently, until the presence of Mr Serle by her side became so distinct to Miss Anning that she could not see the sky, simply, itself, any more, but the sky shored up by the tall body, dark eyes, grey hair, clasped hands, the stern melancholy (but she had been told 'falsely melancholy') face of Roderick Serle, and, knowing how foolish it was, she yet felt impelled to say:

'What a beautiful night!'

Foolish! Idiotically foolish! But if one mayn't be foolish at the age of forty in the presence of the sky, which makes the wisest imbecile – mere wisps of straw – she and Mr Serle atoms, motes, standing there at Mrs Dalloway's window, and their lives, seen by moonlight, as long as an insect's and no more important.

'Well!' said Miss Anning, patting the sofa cushion

emphatically. And down he sat beside her. Was he 'falsely melancholy' as they said? Prompted by the sky, which seemed to make it all a little futile – what they said, what they did – she said something perfectly commonplace again:

'There was a Miss Serle who lived at Canterbury when I was a girl there.'

With the sky in his mind, all the tombs of his ancestors immediately appeared to Mr Serle in a blue romantic light, and his eyes expanding and darkening, he said: 'Yes.'

'We are originally a Norman family, who came over with the Conqueror. That is a Richard Serle buried in the cathedral. He was a Knight of the Garter.'

Miss Anning felt that she had struck accidentally the true man, upon whom the false man was built. Under the influence of the moon (the moon which symbolised man to her, she could see it through a chink of the curtain, and she took dips of the moon) she was capable of saying almost anything and she settled in to disinter the true man who was buried under the false, saying to herself: 'On, Stanley, on' – which was a watch-word of hers, a secret spur, or scourge such as middle-aged people often make to flagellate some inveterate vice, hers being a deplorable timidity, or rather indolence, for it was not so much that she lacked courage, but lacked energy, especially in talking to men, who frightened her rather, and so often her talks petered out into dull commonplaces, and she had very few men friends – very few intimate friends at all, she thought, but after all, did she want them? No. She had Sarah, Arthur, the cottage, the chow and, of course *that*, she thought, dipping herself, sousing herself, even as she sat on the sofa beside Mr Serle, in *that*, in the sense she had coming home of something

35

collected there, a cluster of miracles, which she could not believe other people had (since it was she only who had Arthur, Sarah, the cottage, and the chow), but she soused herself again in the deep satisfactory possession, feeling that what with this and the moon (music that was, the moon), she could afford to leave this man and that pride of his in the Serles buried. No! That was the danger – she must not sink into torpidity – not at her age. 'On, Stanley, on,' she said to herself, and asked him:

'Do you know Canterbury yourself?'

Did he know Canterbury! Mr Serle smiled, thinking how absurd a question it was – how little she knew, this nice quiet woman who played some instrument and seemed intelligent and had good eyes, and was wearing a very nice old necklace – knew what it meant. To be asked if he knew Canterbury. When the best years of his life, all his memories, things he had never been able to tell anybody, but had tried to write – ah, had tried to write (and he sighed) all had centred in Canterbury; it made him laugh.

His sigh and then his laugh, his melancholy, and his humour, made people like him, and he knew it, and yet being liked had not made up for the disappointment, and if he sponged on the liking people had for him (paying long calls on sympathetic ladies, long, long calls), it was half-bitterly, for he had never done a tenth part of what he could have done, and had dreamed of doing, as a boy in Canterbury. With a stranger he felt a renewal of hope because they could not say that he had not done what he had promised, and yielding to his charm would give him a fresh start – at fifty! She had touched the spring. Fields and flowers and grey buildings dripped down into his mind, formed silver drops on the gaunt, dark walls of his mind and dripped down. With such an image his poems often began. He felt the desire to make images now, sitting by this quiet woman.

'Yes, I know Canterbury,' he said reminiscently, sentimentally, inviting, Miss Anning felt, discreet questions, and that was what made him interesting to so many people, and it was this extraordinary facility and responsiveness to talk on his part that had been his undoing, so he thought often, taking his studs out and putting his keys and small change on the dressing-table after one of these parties (and he went out sometimes almost every night in the season), and, going down to breakfast, becoming quite different, grumpy, unpleasant at breakfast to his wife, who was an invalid, and never went out, but had old friends to see her sometimes, women friends for the most part, interested in Indian philosophy and different cures and different doctors, which Roderick Serle snubbed off by some caustic remark too clever for her to meet, except by gentle expostulations and a tear or two – he had failed, he often thought, because he could not cut himself off utterly from society and the company of women, which was so necessary to him, and write. He had involved himself too deep in life – and here he would cross his knees (all his movements were a little unconventional and distinguished) and not blame himself, but put the blame off upon the richness of his nature, which he compared favourably with Wordsworth's, for example, and, since he had given so much to people, he felt, resting his head on his hands, they in their turn should help him, and this was the prelude, tremulous, fascinating, exciting, to talk; and images bubbled up in his mind.

'She's like a fruit tree – like a flowering cherry tree,' he said, looking at a youngish woman with fine white hair. It was a nice sort of image, Ruth Anning thought – rather nice, yet she did not feel sure that she liked this distinguished, melancholy man with his gestures; and it's odd, she thought, how one's feelings are influenced. She did not like *him*, though she rather liked that comparison of his of a woman to a cherry tree. Fibres of her were floated capriciously this way and that, like the tentacles of a sea anemone, how thrilled, now snubbed, and her brain, miles away, cool and distant, up in the air, received messages which it would sum up in time so that, when people talked about Roderick Serle (and he was a bit of a figure) she would say unhesitatingly: 'I like him,' or 'I don't like him,' and her opinion would be made up for ever. An odd thought; a solemn thought; throwing a green light on what human fellowship consisted of.

'It's odd that you should know Canterbury,' said Mr Serle. 'It's always a shock,' he went on (the white-haired lady having passed), 'when one meets someone' (they had never met before), 'by chance, as it were, who touches the fringe of what has meant a great deal to oneself, touches accidentally, for I suppose Canterbury was nothing but a nice old town to you. So you stayed there one summer with an aunt?' (That was all Ruth Anning was going to tell him about her visit to Canterbury.) 'And you saw the sights and went away and never thought of it again.'

Let him think so; not liking him, she wanted him to run away with an absurd idea of her. For really, her three months in Canterbury had been amazing. She remembered to the last detail, though it was merely a chance visit, going to see Miss

Charlotte Serle, an acquaintance of her aunt's. Even now she could respect Miss Serle's very words about the thunder. 'Whenever I wake, or hear thunder in the night, I think "Someone has been killed".' And she could see the hard, hairy, diamond-patterned carpet, and the twinkling, suffused, brown eyes of the elderly lady, holding the teacup out unfilled, while she said that about the thunder. And always she saw Canterbury, all thundercloud and livid apple blossom, and the long grey backs of the buildings.

The thunder roused her from her plethoric middle-aged swoon of indifference; 'On, Stanley, on,' she said to herself; that is, this man shall not glide away from me, like everybody else, on this false assumption; I will tell him the truth.

'I loved Canterbury,' she said.

He kindled instantly. It was his gift, his fault, his destiny.

'Loved it,' he repeated. 'I can see that you did.'

Her tentacles sent back the message that Roderick Serle was nice.

Their eyes met; collided rather, for each felt that behind the eyes the secluded being, who sits in darkness while his shallow agile companion does all the tumbling and beckoning, and keeps the show going, suddenly stood erect; flung off his cloak; confronted the other. It was alarming; it was terrific. They were elderly and burnished into a glowing smoothness, so that Roderick Serle would go, perhaps to a dozen parties in a season, and feel nothing out of the common, or only sentimental regrets, and the desire for pretty images – like this of the flowering cherry tree – and all the time there stagnated in him unstirred a sort of superiority to his company, a sense of untapped resources, which sent him back home dissatisfied with his life, with himself, yawning, empty, capricious. But now, quite suddenly, like a white bolt in a mist (but this image forged itself with the inevitability of lightning and loomed up), there it had happened; the old ecstasy of life; its invincible assault; for it was unpleasant, at the same time that it rejoiced and rejuvenated and filled the veins and nerves with threads of ice and fire; it was terrifying. 'Canterbury twenty years ago,' said Miss Anning, as one lays a shade over an intense light, or covers some burning peach with a green leaf, for it is too strong, too ripe, too full.

Sometimes she wished she had married. Sometimes the cool peace of middle life, with its automatic devices for shielding mind and body from bruises, seemed to her, compared with the thunder and the livid apple-blossom of Canterbury, base. She could imagine something different, more like lightning, more intense. She could imagine some physical sensation. She could imagine –

And, strangely enough, for she had never seen him before, her senses, those tentacles which were thrilled and snubbed, now sent no more messages, now lay quiescent, as if she and Mr Serle knew each other so perfectly, were, in fact, so closely united that they had only to float side by side down this stream.

Of all things, nothing is so strange as human intercourse, she thought, because of its changes, its extraordinary irrationality, her dislike being now nothing short of the most intense and rapturous love, but directly the word 'love' occurred to her, she rejected it, thinking again how obscure the mind was, with its very few words for all these astonishing perceptions, these alternations of pain and pleasure. For how did one name this. That is what she felt now, the withdrawal of human affection,

Serle's disappearance, and the instant need they were both under to cover up what was so desolating and degrading to human nature that everyone tried to bury it decently from sight – this withdrawal, this violation of trust, and seeking some decent and acknowledged and accepted burial form, she said:

'Of course, whatever they may do, they can't spoil Canterbury.'

He smiled; he accepted it; he crossed his knees the other way about. She did her part; he his. So things came to an end. And over them both came instantly that paralysing blankness of feeling, when nothing bursts from the mind, when its walls appear like slate; when vacancy almost hurts, and the eyes petrified and fixed see the same spot – a pattern, a coal scuttle – with an exactness which is terrifying, since no emotion, no idea, no impression of any kind comes to change it, to modify it, to embellish it, since the fountains of feeling seem sealed and as the mind turns rigid, so does the body; stark, statuesque, so that neither Mr Serle nor Miss Anning could move or speak, and they felt as if an enchanter had freed them, and spring flushed every vein with streams of life, when Mira Cartwright, tapping Mr Serle archly on the shoulder, said:

'I saw you at the *Meistersinger,* and you cut me. Villain,' said Miss Cartwright, 'you don't deserve that I should ever speak to you again.'

And they could separate.

6

The New Dress

MABEL HAD HER first serious suspicion that something was wrong as she took her cloak off and Mrs Barnet, while handing her the mirror and touching the brushes and thus drawing her attention, perhaps rather markedly, to all the appliances for tidying and improving hair, complexion, clothes, which existed on the dressing-table, confirmed the suspicion – that it was not right, not quite right, which growing stronger as she went upstairs and springing at her, with conviction as she greeted Clarissa Dalloway, she went straight to the far end of the room, to a shaded corner where a looking-glass hung and looked. No! It was not *right*. And at once the misery which she always tried to hide, the profound dissatisfaction – the sense she had had, ever since she was a child, of being inferior to other people – set upon her, relentlessly, remorselessly, with an intensity which she could not beat off, as she would when she woke at night at home, by reading Borrow or Scott; for oh these men, oh these women, all were thinking – 'What's Mabel wearing? What a fright she looks! What a hideous new dress!' – their eyelids flickering as they came up and then their lids shutting rather tight. It was her own appalling inadequacy; her cowardice; her mean, water-sprinkled blood that depressed her. And at once the whole of the room where, for ever so many hours, she had planned with the little dressmaker how it was to go, seemed sordid, repulsive; and her own drawing-room so shabby, and herself, going out, puffed up with vanity as she touched the letters on the hall table and said: 'How dull!' to show off – all this now seemed unutterably silly, paltry, and provincial. All this had been absolutely destroyed, shown up, exploded, the moment she came into Mrs Dalloway's drawing-room.

What she had thought that evening when, sitting over the teacups, Mrs Dalloway's invitation came, was that, of course, she could not be fashionable. It was absurd to pretend it even – fashion meant cut, meant style, meant thirty guineas at least – but why not be original? Why not be herself, anyhow? And, getting up, she had taken that old fashion book of her mother's, a Paris fashion book of the time of the Empire, and had thought how much prettier, more dignified, and more womanly they were then, and so set herself – oh, it was foolish – trying to be like them, pluming herself in fact, upon being modest and old-fashioned, and very charming, giving herself up, no doubt about it, to an orgy of self-love, which deserved to be chastised, and so rigged herself out like this.

But she dared not look in the glass. She could not face the whole horror – the pale yellow, idiotically old-fashioned silk dress with its long skirt and its high sleeves and its waist and all the things that looked so charming in the fashion book, but not on her, not among all these ordinary people. She felt like a dressmaker's dummy standing there, for young people to stick pins into.

'But, my dear, it's perfectly charming!' Rose Shaw said, looking her up and down with that little satirical pucker of the lips which she expected – Rose herself being dressed in the height of fashion, precisely like everybody else, always.

We are all like flies trying to crawl over the edge of the saucer, Mabel thought, and repeated the phrase as if she were crossing herself, as if she were trying to find some spell to annul this pain, to make this agony endurable. Tags of Shakespeare, lines from books she had read ages ago, suddenly came to her when she was in agony, and she repeated them over and over again. 'Flies trying to crawl,' she repeated. If she could say that over often enough and make herself see the flies, she would become numb, chill, frozen, dumb. Now she could see flies crawling slowly out of a saucer of milk with their wings stuck together; and she strained and strained (standing in front of the looking-glass, listening to Rose Shaw) to make herself see Rose Shaw and all the other people there as flies, trying to hoist themselves out of something, or into something, meagre, insignificant, toiling flies. But she could not see them like that, not other people. She saw herself like that – she was a fly, but the others were dragonflies, butterflies, beautiful insects, dancing, fluttering, skimming, while she alone dragged herself up out of the saucer. (Envy and spite, the most detestable of the vices, were her chief faults.)

'I feel like some dowdy, decrepit, horribly dingy old fly,' she said, making Robert Haydon stop just to hear her say that, just to reassure herself by furbishing up a poor weak-kneed phrase and so showing how detached she was, how witty, that she did not feel in the least out of anything. And, of course, Robert Haydon answered something, quite polite, quite insincere, which she saw through instantly, and said to herself, directly he went (again from some book), 'Lies, lies, lies!' For a party makes things either much more real, or much less real, she thought; she saw in a flash to the bottom of Robert Haydon's heart; she saw through everything. She saw the truth. *This* was true, this drawing-room, this self, the other false. Miss Milan's little workroom was really terribly hot, stuffy, sordid. It smelt of clothes and cabbage cooking; and yet, when Miss Milan put the glass in her hand, and she looked at herself with the dress on, finished, an extraordinary bliss shot through her heart. Suffused with light, she sprang into existence. Rid of cares and wrinkles, what she had dreamed of herself was there – a beautiful woman. Just for a second (she had not dared look longer, Miss Milan wanted to know about the length of the skirt), there looked at her, framed in the scrolloping mahogany, a grey-white, mysteriously smiling, charming girl, the core of herself, the soul of herself; and it was not vanity only, not only self-love that made her think it good, tender, and true. Miss Milan said the skirt could not well be longer; if anything the skirt, said Miss Milan, puckering her forehead, considering with all her wits about her, must be shorter; and she felt, suddenly, honestly, full of love for Miss Milan, much, much fonder of Miss Milan than of anyone in the whole world, and could have cried for pity that she should be crawling on the floor with her mouth full of pins, and her face red and her eyes bulging – that one human being should be doing this for another, and she saw them all as human beings merely, and herself going off to her party, and Miss Milan pulling the cover over the canary's cage, or letting him pick a hemp-seed from between her lips, and the thought of it, of this side of human nature and its patience and its endurance and its being content with such miserable, scanty, sordid, little pleasures filled her eyes with tears.

And now the whole thing had vanished. The dress, the room, the love, the pity, the scrolloping looking-glass, and the canary's cage – all had vanished, and here she was in a corner of Mrs Dalloway's drawing-room, suffering tortures, woken wide awake to reality.

But it was all so paltry, weak-blooded, and petty-minded to care so much at her age with two children, to be still so utterly dependent on people's opinions and not have principles or convictions, not to be able to say as other people did, 'There's Shakespeare! There's death! We're all weevils in a captain's biscuit' – or whatever it was that people did say.

She faced herself straight in the glass; she pecked at her left shoulder; she issued out into the room, as if spears were thrown at her yellow dress from all sides. But instead of looking fierce or tragic, as Rose Shaw would have done – Rose would have looked like Boadicea – she looked foolish and self-conscious, and simpered like a schoolgirl and slouched across the room, positively slinking, as if she were a beaten mongrel, and looked at a picture, an engraving. As if one went to a party to look at a picture! Everybody knew why she did it – it was from shame, from humiliation.

'Now the fly's in the saucer,' she said to herself, 'right in the middle, and can't get out, and the milk,' she thought, rigidly staring at the picture, 'is sticking its wings together.'

'It's so old-fashioned,' she said to Charles Burt, making him stop (which by itself he hated) on his way to talk to someone else.

She meant, or she tried to make herself think that she meant, that it was the picture and not her dress, that was old-fashioned. And one word of praise, one word of affection from Charles would have made all the difference to her at the moment. If he had only said, 'Mabel, you're looking charming to-night!' it would have changed her life. But then she ought to have been truthful and direct. Charles said nothing of the kind, of course. He was malice itself. He always saw through one, especially if one were feeling particularly mean, paltry, or feeble-minded.

'Mabel's got a new dress!' he said, and the poor fly was absolutely shoved into the middle of the saucer. Really, he would like her to drown, she believed. He had no heart, no fundamental kindness, only a veneer of friendliness. Miss Milan was much more real, much kinder. If only one could feel that and stick to it, always. 'Why,' she asked herself – replying to Charles much too pertly, letting him see that she was out of temper, or 'ruffled' as he called it ('Rather ruffled?' he said and went on to laugh at her with some woman over there) – 'Why,' she asked herself, 'can't I feel one thing always, feel quite sure that Miss Milan is right, and Charles wrong and stick to it, feel sure about the canary and pity and love and not be whipped all round in a second by coming into a room full of people?' It was her odious, weak, vacillating character again, always giving at the critical moment and not being seriously interested in conchology, etymology, botany, archaeology, cutting up potatoes and watching them fructify like Mary Dennis, like Violet Searle.

Then Mrs Holman, seeing her standing there, bore down upon her. Of course a thing like a dress was beneath Mrs

Holman's notice, with her family always tumbling downstairs or having the scarlet fever. Could Mabel tell her if Elmthorpe was ever let for August and September? Oh, it was a conversation that bored her unutterably! – it made her furious to be treated like a house agent or a messenger boy, to be made use of. Not to have value, that was it, she thought, trying to grasp something hard, something real, while she tried to answer sensibly about the bathroom and the south aspect and the hot water to the top of the house; and all the time she could see little bits of her yellow dress in the round looking-glass which made them all the size of boot-buttons or tadpoles; and it was amazing to think how much humiliation and agony and self-loathing and effort and passionate ups and downs of feeling were contained in a thing the size of a threepenny bit. And what was still odder, this thing, this Mabel Waring, was separate, quite disconnected; and though Mrs Holman (the black button) was leaning forward and telling her how her eldest boy had strained his heart running, she could see her too, quite detached in the looking-glass, and it was impossible that the black dot, leaning forward, gesticulating, should make the yellow dot, sitting solitary, self-centred, feel what the black dot was feeling, yet they pretended.

'So impossible to keep boys quiet' – that was the kind of thing one said.

And Mrs Holman, who could never get enough sympathy and snatched what little there was greedily, as if it were her right (but she deserved much more for there was her little girl who had come down this morning with a swollen knee-joint), took this miserable offering and looked at it suspiciously, grudgingly, as if it were a halfpenny when it ought to have been a pound and put it away in her purse, must put up with it, mean and miserly though it was, times being hard, so very hard; and on she went, creaking, injured Mrs Holman, about the girl with the swollen joints. Ah, it was tragic, this greed, this clamour of human beings, like a row of cormorants, barking and flapping their wings for sympathy – it was tragic, could one have felt it and not merely pretended to feel it!

But in her yellow dress to-night she could not wring out one drop more; she wanted it all, all for herself. She knew (she kept on looking into the glass, dipping into that dreadfully showing-up blue pool) that she was condemned, despised, left like this in a backwater, because of her being like this, a feeble, vacillating creature; and it seemed to her that the yellow dress was a penance which she had deserved, and if she had been dressed like Rose Shaw, in lovely, clinging green with a ruffle of swansdown, she would have deserved that; and she thought that there was no escape for her – none whatever. But it was not her fault altogether, after all. It was being one of a family of ten; never having money enough, always skimping and paring; and her mother carrying great cans, and the linoleum worn on the stair edges, and one sordid little domestic tragedy after another – nothing catastrophic, the sheep farm failing, but not utterly; her eldest brother marrying beneath him but not very much – there was no romance, nothing extreme about them all. They petered out respectably in seaside resorts; every watering-place had one of her aunts even now asleep in some lodging with the front windows not quite facing the sea. That was like them – they had to squint at things always. And she had done the same – she was just like her aunts. For all her dreams of living in India, married to some hero like Sir Henry

Lawrence, some empire builder (still the sight of a native in a turban filled her with romance), she had failed utterly. She had married Hubert, with his safe, permanent underling's job in the Law Courts, and they managed tolerably in a smallish house, without proper maids, and hash when she was alone or just bread and butter, but now and then – Mrs Holman was off, thinking her the most dried-up, unsympathetic twig she had ever met, absurdly dressed, too, and would tell everyone about Mabel's fantastic appearance – now and then, thought Mabel Waring, left alone on the blue sofa, punching the cushion in order to look occupied, for she would not join Charles Burt and Rose Shaw, chattering like magpies and perhaps laughing at her by the fireplace – now and then, there did come to her delicious moments, reading the other night in bed, for instance, or down by the sea on the sand in the sun, at Easter – let her recall it – a great tuft of pale sand-grass standing all twisted like a shock of spears against the sky, which was blue like a smooth china egg, so firm, so hard, and then the melody of the waves – 'Hush, hush,' they said, and the children's shouts paddling – yes, it was a divine moment, and there she lay, she felt, in the hand of the Goddess who was the world; rather a hard-hearted, but very beautiful Goddess, a little lamb laid on the altar (one did think these silly things, and it didn't matter so long as one never said them). And also with Hubert sometimes she had quite unexpectedly – carving the mutton for Sunday lunch, for no reason, opening a letter, coming into a room – divine moments, when she said to herself (for she would never say this to anybody else), 'This is it. This has happened. This is it!' And the other way about it was equally surprising – that is, when everything was arranged – music, weather, holidays, every reason for happiness was there – then nothing happened at all. One wasn't happy. It was flat, just flat, that was all.

Her wretched self again, no doubt! She had always been a fretful, weak, unsatisfactory mother, a wobbly wife, lolling about in a kind of twilight existence with nothing very clear or very bold, or more one thing than another, like all her brothers and sisters, except perhaps Herbert – they were all the same poor water-veined creatures who did nothing. Then in the midst of this creeping, crawling life, suddenly she was on the crest of a wave. That wretched fly – where had she read the story that kept coming into her mind about the fly and the saucer? – struggled out. Yes, she had those moments. But now that she was forty, they might come more and more seldom. By degrees she would cease to struggle any more. But that was deplorable! That was not to be endured! That made her feel ashamed of herself!

She would go to the London Library to-morrow. She would find some wonderful, helpful, astonishing book, quite by chance, a book by a clergyman, by an American no one had ever heard of; or she would walk down the Strand and drop, accidentally, into a hall where a miner was telling about the life in the pit, and suddenly she would become a new person. She would wear a uniform; she would be called Sister Somebody; she would never give a thought to clothes again. And for ever after she would be perfectly clear about Charles Burt and Miss Milan and this room and that room; and it would be always, day after day, as if she were lying in the sun or carving the mutton. It would be it!

So she got up from the blue sofa, and the yellow button in the looking-glass got up too, and she waved her hand to

Charles and Rose to show them she did not depend on them one scrap, and the yellow button moved out of the looking-glass, and all the spears were gathered into her breast as she walked towards Mrs Dalloway and said 'Good night.'

'But it's too early to go,' said Mrs Dalloway, who was always so charming.

'I'm afraid I must,' said Mabel Waring. 'But,' she added in her weak, wobbly voice which only sounded ridiculous when she tried to strengthen it, 'I have enjoyed myself enormously.'

'I have enjoyed myself,' she said to Mr Dalloway, whom she met on the stairs.

'Lies, lies, lies!' she said to herself, going downstairs, and 'Right in the saucer!' she said to herself as she thanked Mrs Barnet for helping her and wrapped herself, round and round, in the Chinese cloak she had worn these twenty years.

7

A Summing Up

SINCE IT HAD grown hot and crowded indoors, since there could be no danger on a night like this of damp, since the Chinese lanterns seemed hung red and green fruit in the depths of an enchanted forest, Mr Bertram Pritchard led Mrs Latham into the garden.

The open air and the sense of being out of doors bewildered Sasha Latham, the tall, handsome, rather indolent looking lady, whose majesty of presence was so great that people never credited her with feeling perfectly inadequate and gauche when she had to say something at a party. But so it was; and she was glad that she was with Bertram, who could be trusted, even out of doors, to talk without stopping. Written down what he said was in itself insignificant, but there was no connection between the different remarks. Indeed, if one had taken a pencil and written down his very words – and one night of his talk would have filled a whole book – no one could doubt, reading them, that the poor man was intellectually deficient. This was far from the case, for Mr Pritchard was an esteemed civil servant and a Companion of the Bath;

but what was even stranger was that he was almost invariably liked. There was a sound in his voice, some accent of emphasis, some lustre in the incongruity of his ideas, some emanation from his round, chubby brown face and robin redbreast's figure, something immaterial, and unseizable, which existed and flourished and made itself felt independently of his words, indeed, often in opposition to them. This Sasha Latham would be thinking, while he chattered on about his tour in Devonshire, about inns and landladies, about Eddie and Freddie, about cows and night travelling, about cream and stars, about continental railways and Bradshaw, catching cod, catching cold, influenza, rheumatism and Keats – she was thinking of him in the abstract as a person whose existence was good, creating him as he spoke in a guise that was different from what he said, and was certainly the true Bertram Pritchard, even though one could not prove it. How could one prove that he was a loyal friend and very sympathetic and – but here, as so often happened, talking to Bertram Pritchard, she forgot his existence, and began to think of something else.

It was the night she thought of, hitching herself together in some way, taking a look up into the sky. It was the country she smelt suddenly, the sombre stillness of fields under the stars, but here, in Mrs Dalloway's back garden, in Westminster, the beauty, country born and bred as she was, thrilled her because of the contrast presumably; there the smell of hay in the air and behind her the room full of people. She walked with Bertram; she walked rather like a stag, with a little give of the ankles, fanning herself, majestic, silent, with all her senses roused, her ears pricked, snuffing the air, as if she had been some wild, but perfectly controlled creature taking its pleasure by night.

This, she thought, is the greatest of marvels; the supreme achievement of the human race. Where there were osier beds and coracles paddling through a swamp, there is this; and she thought of the dry, thick, well-built house, stored with valuables, humming with people coming close to each other, going away from each other, exchanging their views, stimulating each other. And Clarissa Dalloway had made it open in the wastes of the night, had laid paving stones over the bog, and, when they came to the end of the garden (it was in fact extremely small), and she and Bertram sat down on deck chairs, she looked at the house veneratingly, enthusiastically, as if a golden shaft ran through her and tears formed on it and fell in profound thanksgiving. Shy though she was and almost incapable when suddenly presented to someone of saying anything, fundamentally humble, she cherished a profound admiration for other people. To be them would be marvellous, but she was condemned to be herself and could only in this silent enthusiastic way, sitting outside in a garden, applaud the society of humanity from which she was excluded. Tags of poetry in praise of them rose to her lips; they were adorable and good, above all courageous, triumphers over night and fens, the survivors, the company of adventurers who, set about with dangers, sail on.

By some malice of fate she was unable to join, but she could sit and praise while Bertram chattered on, he being among the voyagers, as cabin boy or common seaman – someone who ran up masts, gaily whistling. Thinking thus, the branch of some tree in front of her became soaked and steeped in her admiration for the people of the house; dripped gold; or stood sentinel erect. It was part of the gallant and carousing company, a mast from which the flag streamed. There was a barrel of some kind against the wall, and this, too, she endowed.

Suddenly Bertram, who was restless physically, wanted to explore the grounds, and, jumping on to a heap of bricks, he peered over the garden wall. Sasha peered over too. She saw a bucket or perhaps a boot. In a second the illusion vanished. There was London again; the vast inattentive impersonal world; motor omnibuses; affairs; lights before public-houses; and yawning policemen.

Having satisfied his curiosity, and replenished, by a moment's silence, his bubbling fountains of talk, Bertram invited Mr and Mrs Somebody to sit with them, pulling up two more chairs. There they sat again, looking at the same house, the same tree, the same barrel; only having looked over the wall and had a glimpse of the bucket, or rather of London going its ways unconcernedly, Sasha could no longer spray over the world that cloud of gold. Bertram talked and the Somebodies – for the life of her she could not remember if they were called Wallace or Freeman – answered, and all their words passed through a thin haze of gold and fell into prosaic daylight. She looked at the dry, thick Queen Anne House; she did her best to remember what she had read at school about the Isle of Thorney and men in coracles, oysters, and wild duck and mists, but it seemed to her a logical affair of drains and carpenters, and this party – nothing but people in evening dress.

Then she asked herself, which view is the true one? She could see the bucket and the house half lit up, half unlit.

She asked this question of that somebody whom, in her

humble way, she had composed out of the wisdom and power of other people. The answer came often by accident – she had known her old spaniel answer by wagging his tail.

Now the tree, denuded of its gilt and majesty, seemed to supply her with an answer; became a field tree – the only one in a marsh. She had often seen it; seen the red-flushed clouds between its branches, or the moon split up, darting irregular flashes of silver. But what answer? Well that the soul – for she was conscious of a movement in her of some creature beating its way about her and trying to escape which momentarily she called the soul – is by nature unmated, a widow bird; a bird perched aloof on that tree.

But then Bertram, putting his arm through hers in his familiar way, for he had known her all her life, remarked that they were not doing their duty and must go in.

At that moment, in some back street or public-house, the usual terrible sexless, inarticulate voice rang out; a shriek, a cry. And the widow bird, startled, flew away, describing wider and wider circles until it became (what she called her soul) remote as a crow which has been startled up into the air by a stone thrown at it.

THE HISTORY OF VINTAGE

The famous American publisher Alfred A. Knopf (1892–1984) founded Vintage Books in the United States in 1954 as a paperback home for the authors published by his company. Vintage was launched in the United Kingdom in 1990 and works independently from the American imprint although both are part of the international publishing group, Random House.

Vintage in the United Kingdom was initially created to publish paperback editions of books acquired by the prestigious hardback imprints in the Random House Group such as Jonathan Cape, Chatto & Windus, Hutchinson and later William Heinemann, Secker & Warburg and The Harvill Press. There are many Booker and Nobel Prize-winning authors on the Vintage list and the imprint publishes a huge variety of fiction and non-fiction. Over the years Vintage has expanded and the list now includes great authors of the past – who are published under the Vintage Classics imprint – as well as many of the most influential authors of the present.

For a full list of the books Vintage publishes, please visit our website
www.vintage-books.co.uk

For book details and other information about the classic authors we publish, please visit the Vintage Classics website
www.vintage-classics.info

www.vintage-classics.info